… for a bird of the air shall carry
the voice, and that which hath
wings shall tell the matter.

ECCLESIASTES, 10: 20

For my friends and fellow
journeymen: Ben, Pomme,
Daniel and TUUP
— H. L.

Barefoot Books
37 West 17th Street
4th Floor East
New York, New York 10011

First published in the United States of America in 2000 by Barefoot Books, Inc.

This book is printed on 100% acid-free paper

The main text has been typeset in Perpetua
The illustrations were prepared in watercolor on paper

Graphic design by Design Principals, England
Color separation by Grafiscan, Italy
Printed in Hong Kong/China by South China Printing Co. (1988) Ltd.

1 3 5 7 9 8 6 4 2

U.S. Cataloging-in-Publication Data (Library of Congress Standards)

Lupton, Hugh.
        The songs of birds / retold by Hugh Lupton ; illustrated by Steve
Palin.—1st ed.
[80]p. : col. ill. ;   cm.
Summary: A varied collection of bird stories and poems from around the
world. Drawn from oral traditions that stretch back to ancient times.
ISBN 1-84148-045-2
1. Birds — Stories. 2. Birds — Poetry. I. Palin, Steve, ill. II. Title.
        808.819 —dc21 2000 AC   CIP

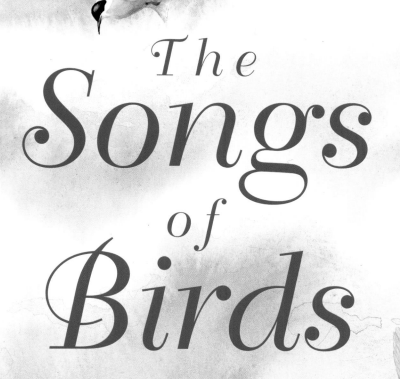

The Songs of Birds

Stories and Poems from Many Cultures

Collected and retold by
HUGH LUPTON

Illustrated by
STEVE PALIN

walk
the way of wonder...
Barefoot Books

Contents

Introduction

Birds had achieved their perfection, they had evolved into the forms and shapes we know today, long before humankind came into being. Our earliest ancestors would have seen the quick azure flight of the kingfisher, the slow circling of ravens, and the arrow formations of geese against the sky, just as we do today. Their ears would have rung with the screeching of gulls, the chattering of sparrows and the liquid song of nightingales. Their sense of the shifting of the seasons would have been attuned to the arrival of the cuckoo and the departure of swallows. The Paleolithic hunters of forty thousand years ago would have marveled at the mud architecture of a dipper's nest or the tiny perfection of a wren's.

Birds have flitted and soared, dived and perched, they have whistled and sung, honked and hooted within the sight and hearing of countless generations of people — leaving ancient images and echoes that are constantly renewed and are inherited by us all. Jacquetta Hawkes, in her wonderful, neglected book *A Land*, has written:

"Once in the spring I stood at the edge of some Norfolk plowland listening to the mating calls of the plovers that were tumbling ecstatically above the fields. The delicious effusions of turtledoves bubbled from a coppice at my back. It seemed to me that I had my ear to a great spiral shell and that these sounds rose from it. The shell was the vortex of time, and as the birds themselves took shape, species after species, so their distinctive songs were formed within them and had been spiraling up ever since. Now, at the very lip of the shell, they reached my present ear."

The stories and poems in this collection are drawn from the oral traditions of many parts of the world. Like the songs of birds, they would have been familiar to our ancestors and they are still told and sung today. In them we glimpse the close connection between birds and the men and women who share their world. These stories and poems are part of a long interaction, one that has existed for many thousands of years, between human speech and birdsong, between human activity and bird flight, and between human understanding and bird teaching.

The Golden-Eye Hatches the World

FINNISH

In the beginning there was water.

In the beginning there was nothing but gray water, and flying over the water there was a golden-eye.

She was looking for somewhere to build her nest. She flew east and west; there was nowhere.

She flew north and south; there was no speck or spit of land. There was only wind and wave.

The mother of the water took pity on the bird. The mother of the water raised her knee above the surface of the water.

Like a bank of sand, the knee of the mother of the water rose up above the waves.

The golden-eye landed on the knee. It seemed a good place; she made her nest there.

She laid seven eggs: six were golden, the last was iron. She settled down on her nest. She brooded for a day; the eggs of gold and iron were warm.

She brooded for a second day; the eggs of gold and iron were hot.

She brooded for a third day; the eggs of gold and iron were burning the leg of the mother of the water. They were scorching her skin. She felt as though her sinews were melting in a terrible fire. The mother of the water could bear it no longer.

She twitched her knee.

The golden-eye flew up into the air and the eggs smashed into the sea. With a hiss of steam the mother of the water lowered her leg down into the gray waves.

The golden-eye was circling in the air, calling and crying to her broken eggs.

But a beautiful thing was happening.

A strange and beautiful thing was taking place.

The broken eggs were becoming a world.

The lower half of one egg became the world beneath, the top half of another became the sky above. The golden yolk of one became the shining sun, the white of another became the pale moon. A mottled shell became the stars in the sky. The dark shards of the iron shell became the dark clouds.

The golden-eye was circling the air inside a world of her own making.

And the mother of the sea rose up and saw this new world. She swung her hand through the waves and arranged the headlands, she made the coasts smooth with the underside of her arm, she lifted lands and continents, she sunk her heel into the deep hollows.

The golden-eye circled in the air above her and the wind whistled in her wings.

That was how our world began.

The Eagle Above Us

CORA

he lives in the sky
far above us
the eagle
looks good there
has a good grip on his world

his world wrapt in gray
but a living, a humid
a beautiful gray

there he glides in the sky
very far
right above us

waits for what Tetewan
netherworld goddess
has to say

bright
his eye
on his world

bright
his eye
on the water of life
the sea
embracing
the earth

frightful his face
radiant his eye
the sun

his feet a deep red
there he is
right above us

spreading his wings
he remembers
who dwell down below

among whom the gods
let rain fall, let dew fall
for life on their earth

there above us he speaks
we can hear him
his words make great sound

deep down they go
where mother Tetewan hears
him and answers
we can hear her

here they meet
her words and the eagle's
we hear them together
together they make great sound

eagle words
fading
far above the water of life

mother words
from deep down
sighing away through the vaults of the sky

The Pigeon, the Sparrow-Hawk and the Theft of Fire

AUSTRALIAN ABORIGINAL

In the beginning the world was cold.

Bitterly cold it was in those early days, and the people had no fire.

They had no fire to crouch beside in the icy weather, no fire to give light in the long darkness of night, no fire to cook their meat or the roots and berries they had gathered.

The only one who had fire was Meeka, the moon, and he kept it in his tail. He wouldn't share his fire; he looked down at the people and he had no pity. He made his way across the sky with his tail burning like a comet - and he kept it all for himself.

One time Wata the pigeon was speaking to his nephew Kwetalbur the sparrow-

hawk: "These are hard times for the world, hard and bitter times. You and I will make a journey together. When the day comes and Meeka is resting, we will take his fire and share it out among the people."

Kwetalbur nodded. "Just call, uncle, and I will come with you."

So the next day, when the sun had risen and the moon was resting, Wata called to Kwetalbur: "Croo-Croo Cru."

Together they flew up into the sky until they came to the place where Meeka had built his shelter. He was asleep, curled around the burning fire in his tail. His spears and spear thrower, his knives and boomerangs were laid out close to hand. He was sucking the air as he breathed: "Hsssssss, hssssssssss."

Wata the pigeon crept closer and closer. He stepped over boomerangs, spears and knives. He seized the fire from Meeka's tail and with a clattering of wings he flew away.

Something had interrupted Meeka's dream. He woke up; he rubbed his eyes. His fire was gone! He looked this way and that way.

There were the thieves! Over there!

He grabbed his weapons and ran after them, hurling spear after spear.

But Wata and Kwetalbur were too fast. They were flying down to the world. They were throwing the fire from beak to beak, throwing and catching the stolen fire as the moon's spears whistled past them.

When they reached the tops of the trees, they put fire into them so that they blazed like flaming torches.

And when the people saw the burning trees, they came running and dancing and shouting: "Look! Wata and Kwetalbur have brought us fire! We will never feel the bitter cold again!"

Pigeon and sparrow-hawk flew from tree to tree, putting fire into each one of them. They put plenty of fire into the she-oaks, the jamwoods and the blackboy trees.

But Meeka, the moon, was still following them.

"Give me back my fire!" he shouted. "I am cold, cold!"

When he saw he couldn't catch them or kill them, and when he saw that the whole world was flickering red and yellow with stolen fire, he gave up the chase. He climbed back into the sky, he called all the clouds and he told them to rain. He told them to rain and rain until the world was covered with water and every fire was drowned.

And so a great flood came.

But Wata the pigeon and Kwetalbur the sparrow-hawk had been clever; they had put fire into the trees. They had put the stolen fire into the wood of the trees. So when the waters of the great flood had dried and drained away, they showed the people how to take the fire out of wood.

They showed the people how to make fire-sticks from she-oaks and jamwoods and blackboy trees. They showed them how to rub the sticks together until fire came. And from that day to this, there has been fire inside wood.

From that day to this, the people have had fire to crouch beside in the icy weather, to give light in the long darkness of night, to cook the meat they have hunted and the roots and berries they have gathered.

And from that day to this, as the women light their fires and watch the gray-blue smoke rise up into the sky, they sing:

"See the smoke of the fire,
the fire that Wata and Kwetalbur brought us;
see the smoke of the fire!"

And as for Meeka, the moon, he has shone pale and cold in the sky since that time, and his blazing tail has disappeared.

The Birds of Rhiannon

CELTIC

… and the birds of Rhiannon came

circling and singing over the sea.

It was a music that could wake the dead

and lull the living to sleep.

One bird was blue with a crimson head,

the second was crimson with a green head,

the third was speckled with a golden head.

The first sang of victory in defeat,

the second sang of defeat in victory,

and the third sang of the freedom of the heart from bondage.

16

The Swallow and the Snake

PALESTINIAN

In the beginning there was God and the Devil.

In the very beginning there was God and the Devil, and there was the world that God had created.

In the center of the world was Paradise: the Garden of Eden. It was God's favorite place with its fruit trees and birdsong, its angels and animals, its dappled paths that he loved to tread in the cool of the evening. He'd even put his newest creatures, man and woman, there for safekeeping.

Now, God didn't want any trouble in Paradise, so he decided to order the Devil to leave.

"The rest of the world is at your disposal," he said, "but Paradise is out of bounds."

The Devil was banished and the gates of Paradise were closed behind him. Of course, as soon as he was outside, the Devil wanted to get back inside.

He searched the walls for a crack or a hole that he could squeeze through, but there was no way back. Then he went to each of the animals and birds and asked them if they would help him get back to Paradise. Each one of them shook its head and refused to help.

Then, at last, the Devil met the snake.

"Listen," he said, "if you'll help me to get back into Paradise, I'll give you the sweetest flesh on earth as your food."

"Well," replied the snake, "what is the sweetest flesh on earth?"

The Devil crouched down and whispered into the snake's ear: "The sweetest flesh on earth is the flesh of Adam and the sons of Adam and the flesh of Eve and the daughters of Eve."

The snake thought about this for a while, then it nodded its thin head up and down.

"Very well," it hissed, "I'll agree to that."

So the Devil (who is infinitely clever) shrank himself, until he was small enough to climb into the snake's mouth, and he crouched behind one of the snake's fangs.

The snake slid through the gates of Paradise; it slid through the lush green grass of Paradise until (by chance or design) it met Eve.

And everyone knows what happened next.

Eve was persuaded to pick the fruit of the tree of the knowledge of good and evil, and she gave some of it to Adam … and all the time it wasn't the snake that was doing the talking; it was the Devil, crouched behind the fang inside the snake's mouth.

And, of course, soon enough God discovered what had happened and Devil, snake, Eve and Adam were banished, and the golden gates of Paradise were closed behind them.

Well, the Devil made off in one direction, Adam and Eve made off in another, and the snake started thinking to itself: "Maybe I should go and claim the sweetest flesh on earth as my food. After all, I've earned it."

The more the snake thought about it, the better the idea seemed to be. And so one day it set off, sliding through the grass towards the house that Adam and Eve had built for themselves.

But at that moment a swallow was flying overhead and he saw the snake just as it was beginning to slither over the threshold of Adam's door.

He swooped down and fluttered over the snake's head.

"Stop!" he said, and the snake stopped.

Now, everyone knows that the swallow is a friend of humankind; he builds his nest in the shadow of our houses even today, just as he did in the time of Adam. But the snake, because it kept its head in the grass, knew nothing about that, and it looked up at the swallow.

"Stop!" said the swallow. "How do you know that the sweetest flesh on earth is the flesh of humans?"

And the snake replied: "Because the Devil told me so."

The swallow began to laugh: "Ha, ha, ha, ha! But the Devil is the Devil. How do you know that he was speaking the truth?"

All this time Adam had been sitting inside his house and he'd overheard this conversation. He got to his feet and came to the doorway.

"Listen, snake," he said, "there's only one way to find out who has the sweetest flesh on earth. I'll send out the mosquito to taste and sample the blood of every single living creature. When she returns, we'll have a great assembly of all the animals and birds, and whoever she says tastes sweetest will be your food from that day onwards."

The snake thought about that for a while, then it nodded its thin head up and down: "Very well, I'll agree to that."

So off went the mosquito, flying north, south, east and west, sucking and sampling the blood of every living creature on earth.

When a year was over she returned.

But the swallow had been watching and waiting, and when he saw the mosquito flying towards the great assembly of animals and birds, he swooped down out of the sky.

"Stop!" he said. "Stop and tell me who has the sweetest flesh on earth."

And the mosquito replied: "To tell you the truth, the sweetest flesh on earth is indeed the flesh of Adam and the sons of Adam and the flesh of Eve and the daughters of Eve."

The swallow fluttered closer to the mosquito: "I'm sorry, I'm just a little deaf. I didn't quite hear what you said."

The mosquito opened her mouth wider to speak louder than before: "THE SWEETEST FLESH ON EARTH IS…"

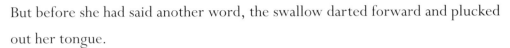

But before she had said another word, the swallow darted forward and plucked out her tongue.

So when the mosquito came to the great assembly of the animals and birds, all she could say was: "Nnnnnnnnnnnnnnnnnnnnnnnnn."

The animals and birds looked at one another. They shook their heads and shrugged their shoulders. Not one of them could understand what the mosquito was trying to tell them.

Then the swallow swooped down out of the sky and perched on Adam's shoulder.

"Fellow creatures," said the bird, "the mosquito is my dear friend."

The animals and birds looked at one another and nodded.

"It's true," they said, "wherever you see a mosquito there's a swallow not far behind."

"The mosquito is my dear friend," said the swallow, "and before she had the terrible misfortune to lose her tongue, she confided in me, and she told me that the sweetest flesh on earth is the flesh of the frog."

And so it was agreed, among all the animals and birds, that from that day onwards the snake should eat the flesh of the frog.

But the snake saw that it had been tricked and it was furious. It uncoiled itself and, quick as a whiplash, it snapped at the swallow.

The swallow flew up into the air … but he wasn't quite quick enough and the jaws of the snake closed around his tail.

And so it was and so it is, from that day to this, that all swallows have had forked tails.

And so it was and so it is, from that day to this, that all snakes have eaten the flesh of the frog.

And so it was and so it is, from that day to this, that all mosquitoes have said
nothing but: "Nnnnnnnnnnnnnnnnnn."

But the mosquito knows that the sweetest flesh on earth is the flesh of
humankind, and she helps herself whenever she can.

And as for us, as for humankind, ever since that time, when we've seen the first
swallow of spring scything the air above our heads, our hearts have lifted as
though an old friend has returned.

Chicken

YORUBA

One who sees corn and is glad.

Happily eating the worm

unaware of her fate.

Every fool will be buried in the cheek.

The foolish chicken has many relatives:

oil is her uncle on the mother's side

pepper and onion are her aunts on the father's side

pounded yam is her in-law.

If she does not see her friend salt for a day

she does not sleep peacefully.

The Raven and the Whale

INUIT

One time Chulyen the raven was eating fish.

The more fish he ate, the hungrier he seemed to become.

"If only there was something that would satisfy this groaning ache of hunger in my belly."

Just then he looked out to sea. A herd of whales was passing, a great school of whales, lifting and rolling in the water, lashing their tails.

"If I was to eat a whale, who knows, maybe I'd get enough meat to satisfy me and smoothen out these troublesome wrinkles of hunger."

Chulyen opened his blue-black wings and flew over the waves. He circled in the air above the whales, flapping his wings and pondering.

Suddenly one of the whales flung itself up out of the water. It opened its mouth, it swallowed Chulyen, it crashed down into the sea.

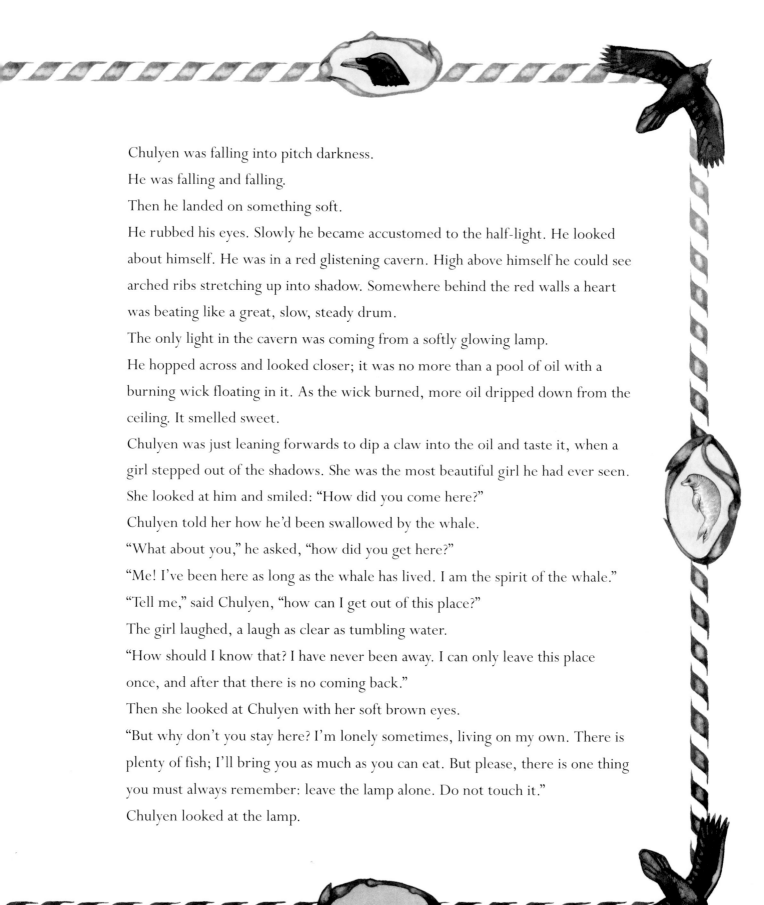

Chulyen was falling into pitch darkness.

He was falling and falling.

Then he landed on something soft.

He rubbed his eyes. Slowly he became accustomed to the half-light. He looked about himself. He was in a red glistening cavern. High above himself he could see arched ribs stretching up into shadow. Somewhere behind the red walls a heart was beating like a great, slow, steady drum.

The only light in the cavern was coming from a softly glowing lamp.

He hopped across and looked closer; it was no more than a pool of oil with a burning wick floating in it. As the wick burned, more oil dripped down from the ceiling. It smelled sweet.

Chulyen was just leaning forwards to dip a claw into the oil and taste it, when a girl stepped out of the shadows. She was the most beautiful girl he had ever seen. She looked at him and smiled: "How did you come here?"

Chulyen told her how he'd been swallowed by the whale.

"What about you," he asked, "how did you get here?"

"Me! I've been here as long as the whale has lived. I am the spirit of the whale."

"Tell me," said Chulyen, "how can I get out of this place?"

The girl laughed, a laugh as clear as tumbling water.

"How should I know that? I have never been away. I can only leave this place once, and after that there is no coming back."

Then she looked at Chulyen with her soft brown eyes.

"But why don't you stay here? I'm lonely sometimes, living on my own. There is plenty of fish; I'll bring you as much as you can eat. But please, there is one thing you must always remember: leave the lamp alone. Do not touch it."

Chulyen looked at the lamp.

"Why not?"

"Because the flame that burns is the life of the whale. If it were to be disturbed, it would be dangerous for the whale…and for you."

So Chulyen gave his word that he would not touch the lamp. The girl smiled at him, then she turned and disappeared among the shadows.

As soon as she was gone, he licked his lips.

"A promise given is a promise kept; I won't touch the lamp."

He looked up at the ceiling where the oil was gathering on a red ridge of flesh, then dripping down into the pool below. He reached out and caught a drop as it fell. He licked it with his tongue.

"Mmmm, delicious - sweet whale oil!"

He caught another drop and swallowed it.

Then, sooner than he'd expected, the girl was back with her arms full of fresh fish. She threw them down on to the floor. Chulyen took his fire-sticks from under his wing and he made a blaze; there was plenty of driftwood lying about. Soon the fish were cooking in the flames. Chulyen and the girl ate the fish; they talked and they laughed. After a while she got to her feet, she smiled at him and she disappeared.

Chulyen went back to the lamp and he drank some more of the sweet, sweet whale oil.

And so it continued for several days: the fish, the oil, the beautiful girl…more fish, more oil. But it wasn't long before Chulyen was bored. There was nothing to do down there in the whale's belly, and the fish and oil only seemed to make those wrinkles of hunger more agonizing than before. They only reminded him how much more he needed to eat.

One time, when he and the girl had finished eating and she had left him alone, he

opened his blue-black wings and flew up to the ceiling of the whale's belly. He examined the place that the oil was coming from.

The drip, drip, drip of it seemed pitifully slow.

He reached with his claw and tore into the ridge of flesh.

A sudden shudder went through the body of the whale.

Chulyen didn't notice. The oil was coming faster. It was mixed with the red of the whale's blood. He flew back down and thrust his head under the flow of delicious, rich, sweet oil. He opened his beak and drank it down. He gulped and gurgled with happiness.

He didn't notice that the great drum of the heart was beating fast and then slow.

The oil was trickling down the sides of his face, his neck and body were sticky with it. Chulyen had never been so happy.

He didn't notice that the pool of oil was drying up and the flame on the wick was getting fainter.

He didn't notice that the heartbeat was slow and faint.

He gulped and gulped and gulped it down.

Then the flame went out and everything was pitch dark.

Suddenly a great convulsion shook the whale's body, then another. Chulyen was tossed about inside the belly of the whale like a seed in a rattle. The enormous body twisted and rolled. Chulyen was thrown this way and that way until he was battered half senseless. For hour after hour he was hurled from side to side. Then everything went still.

Chulyen was lying on his back in pitch darkness. He called to the girl: "Hey! Where are you?"

There was no answer. She had gone. She wouldn't be coming back.

He groped in the darkness for the wick of the lamp, so that he could light it again…but there was no sign of it.

Everything was quiet. Chulyen thought: "Maybe this is what death is like."

Then he heard voices. He heard the sound of laughter, the sound of knives and axes cutting and hacking and slicing into flesh.

Suddenly Chulyen understood what had happened. The body of the whale had been washed ashore by a great storm and now people had found it and they were helping themselves to the meat.

Chulyen was furious. People were helping themselves to the meat of his whale. They were taking his meat for their own use. How dare they!

He crouched in the darkness until the hacking stopped and the voices grew faint. He guessed they were carrying the meat back to their village.

As soon as he was sure the people had gone, Chulyen began to cut a hole in the side of the whale. With his beak and claws he cut through flesh and blubber and skin and pushed his way out into the sunlight. He blinked a few times then looked at the place where the people had been cutting away the meat.

"Huh, they've taken enough; they won't take any more."

He tilted his head to one side and then to the other. Then he had an idea.

He reached through the hole he'd just made and threw his fire-sticks into the belly of the whale, then he opened his blue-black wings and flew up into the sky.

He circled around a few times, watching and waiting.

It wasn't long before the people returned with their knives and axes to take some more of the meat.

Chulyen flapped down and perched on the flank of the dead whale.

The people saw him: "Greetings, Raven. Look at the great gift the sea has brought to our people!"

Chulyen nodded his head up and down: "It is a fine gift, and what is more, I've come to help you cut and carry the meat before it spoils."

Chulyen flapped down to the ground. He showed the people how to peel away the skin and lay it on the ground. He showed them how to pile the chunks of meat on to the skin, so that it could all be dragged to the village in one journey. All morning Chulyen worked with the people and soon there was a mountain of meat stacked on the gray whale-skin.

Then, suddenly, one of the men shouted: "Look! Come and look at this!"

The others looked up from their work: "What's the matter?"

"There are fire-sticks! There are fire-sticks in the belly of the whale!"

Soon all the people were pressing and peering through the ribs into the whale's belly. Chulyen flapped his wings and flew up on to the whale's head.

"Oh dear," he said, "oh dear; it is a bad thing."

The people looked up at him.

"What do you mean, a bad thing, Raven?"

Chulyen shuddered.

"Fire-sticks in a whale's belly, it is a very bad thing."

"Tell us more."

The people were all looking at Chulyen; they were worried now.

Chulyen shuddered again.

"It has been said…but no, it would frighten you."

"Tell us, Raven, you must tell us the truth!"

"Are you sure you want to hear?"

"Yes!"

"It has been said by the wise that fire-sticks found in the belly of a whale will bring certain death to all those who have taken meat from it."

The people backed away from the whale, anyone holding meat in his hands dropped it onto the shingle.

"What sort of death, how will we die, Raven?"

Chulyen threw back his head and shrieked, his whole body was shaking.

"I don't know, I don't want to know, and I'm not going to stay here and find out."

He opened his blue-black wings, he flapped up into the sky and flew away over the sea…but after a little while, he turned and began to fly back again. Just as he'd hoped, the people were running away to their village as fast as their trembling legs would carry them, without looking once over their shoulders.

As soon as they were out of sight, Chulyen landed on the whale.

He fetched his fire-sticks out of the belly and kindled a fire. Soon he was roasting the meat and eating it. He ate and he ate until the mountain of meat piled up on the skin was gone. He ate and he ate until the bones of the whale were picked clean. He ate and he ate until his belly was smoothened and swollen, without a wrinkle of hunger to trouble him.

He ate and he ate until he could eat no more.

And when, several days later, the people of the village plucked up courage to return to the whale, all that was left of it were the clean white bones rattling in the surf at the edge of the sea – and Chulyen was gone.

Song for the Vulture Dance

ORISSA

Golden vulture
Silver vulture
With ungainly hop
She devours the corpse
Golden vulture
Silver vulture
With exploring bill
She pulls out the offal
Golden vulture

Silver vulture
Flapping her wings
She pecks the eyes
Golden vulture
Silver vulture
She breaks the rai-tree
And drinks the sweet juice
Golden vulture
Silver vulture.

The King of the Birds

WELSH

One time the birds were arguing about who should be their king.

"It should be me," said the cockerel. "I've got the loudest voice."

"It should be me," said the heron. "I've got the longest legs."

"It should be me," said the magpie. "I've got the loveliest feathers."

"Stop all this arguing!" said the owl. "Stop all this arguing and listen to me. There is only one way to decide. Whoever can fly the highest will be king."

This was a good idea.

Straight away there was a clattering of wings against the air and a great cloud of birds rose up from the ground.

The cockerel flew as high as the rooftops.

The heron flew as high as the treetops.

The magpie struggled up and up until his beautiful pied wings could carry him no higher, and then he fluttered down to the world.

It was the lark who flew the highest of the little birds, and danced for a while, spilling his song out across the sky.

But it was the eagles who flew the highest of all, circling and slicing the air with their wings…until one after another they fell away too, and only one bird was left.

It was the golden eagle, the great golden eagle.

He looked down at the world far, far, far below.

"I am the king of the birds," he whispered to himself. "I am the mighty king of all the birds."

"Oh no, you're not!"

There was a tiny voice above him. He looked up.

"Oh no, you're not!"

It was the wren, the little jenny wren, smallest of the birds. She had hidden on the eagle's back, tucked between his shoulders as he flew up into the sky, and now she was fluttering above his head.

"I flew the highest! I'm the queen of all the birds!"

The golden eagle was angry, he was furious. He tried to fly up and snatch the little bird out of the sky, but he was too tired, he could fly no higher.

With a sigh he swooped down, and the little jenny wren tumbled down after him.

Soon they were standing before the owl.

"I flew the highest," said the wren.

The owl turned his head and looked at the golden eagle with his round eyes.

"Is she speaking the truth?"

"Yes, she is, but …"

"But what?"

"Yes, she is, but she is a cheat."

There was a great commotion among the birds: "A cheat? A cheat!"

"Yes," said the eagle. "When I flew up into the sky, she was hiding between my shoulders. When I could fly no further, she fluttered up above my head — and now she calls herself queen of all the birds. She's a cheat!"

The birds seized the jenny wren in their claws: "A cheat, a cheat, a cheat!"

"If she's a cheat," said the owl, "then she must die."

He looked this way and that way with his round eyes, and he saw a little cup lying on the ground.

"We'll drown her in that cup."

The birds said: "But the cup is empty."

"Then we will fill it with our tears!"

The birds were so angry that it wasn't difficult for them to weep.

Each of them leaned over the cup and let their tears splash down into it: cockerel tears, heron tears, magpie tears, lark tears. Soon the cup was half full: sparrow tears, swallow tears, robin tears, goose tears.

Last of all it was the owl's turn.

He hopped across to the little cup that was brimming full with the tears of all the birds. He lifted his foot to hold it steady.

He leaned forwards: PLOP…PLOP…PLOP…he dropped three tears into the cup. Then he turned to hop away. But as he turned, one of his claws caught the rim of the cup. It tipped and all the tears of all the birds spilled out onto the grass and soaked into the ground.

When the birds saw what the owl had done, they were angry. They were so angry that they forgot about the wren. They let go of her and they flew at the owl.

"You clumsy bird!"

They mobbed him and pecked him and chased him away.

As soon as they were gone, little jenny wren dived into the nearest hawthorn hedge, and when the other birds returned, she was nowhere to be seen.

And that is why, even to this day, the jenny wren and her husband are queen and king of all the birds.

And that is why the owl flies only in the dusk and the darkness of night, because if the other birds catch sight of him, they remember their spilled tears and they mob him and chase him away.

Bird Song

COPPER ESKIMO

The great gull hovers
on wings spread wide
above us, above us.
He stares, I shout!
His head is white,
his beak gapes,
his small round eyes
look far, look sharp!
Qutiuk! Qutiuk!

The great skua hovers
on wings spread wide
above us, above us.
He stares, I shout!
His head is black,
his beak gapes,
his small round eyes
look far, look sharp!
Ijoq! Ijoq!

The great raven hovers
on wings spread wide
above us, above us.
He stares, I shout!
His head is blue-black,
his beak is sharp
(does it have teeth?)
His eyes squint!
Qara! Qara!

And then there is the owl,
the great owl!
He hovers
on wings spread wide
above us, above us.
He stares, I shout!
His head is swollen,
his beak is hooked,
and his round eyes
have lids turned inside out,
red and heavy!
Oroq! Oroq!

The Eagle and the Child

BAILA

There was once a woman. She was working in the fields.

She was hoeing the brown earth. On her back she was carrying a baby.

Suddenly the baby began to cry.

She lifted it from her back, held it to her breast and suckled it.

Soon the baby was sleeping. She carried it across and laid it down on the soft grass at the edge of the field, in the shade of a tree.

Then she returned to work, scratching and scratching at the brown earth with her hoe. After a while the baby began to cry again.

She thought: "I'll leave it for a while."

She carried on hoeing without looking over her shoulder.

Then the crying stopped and the child began to laugh, a gurgling laugh of

contentment and pleasure. The woman turned and saw that an eagle had perched
by the child. It was soothing her baby with its wings.

She thought: "The eagle is eating my child! How terrible!"

She ran across the field, waving her hoe in the air.

The eagle flew away. She picked up the baby; it was unharmed. She put it onto
her back again and at the end of the day she returned to her village.

She told nobody of the marvel she had seen, not even her husband.

The next day she was working in the field again. As before, she suckled the baby
and laid it on the soft grass. The baby began to laugh; she turned and saw the
eagle again. It was neither biting nor scratching; it was rustling its feathers and
swinging its head from side to side. The baby was reaching up with its little
hands and chortling with pleasure.

The woman thought: "This is a great marvel!"
She walked slowly towards the eagle. As she
drew close, it beat its wings against the air
and flew away. It circled and then perched
in the branches of a tree and looked at her.
The woman picked up the baby and ran back
to the village. She found her husband and
she told him about everything she had seen.
Her husband laughed: "You are lying – such
a thing could never take place."

His wife said no more. She turned on her heel
and walked back to the field. She laid the baby
on the soft grass in the shade of the tree and set to
work with her hoe. After a while the baby cried.

She stood and watched as the eagle flew down. She watched it fan out its wings and tenderly play with the child.

The woman dropped her hoe, lifted her skirts and ran to the village.

"Husband! Husband! You called me a liar. Come and see whether or not I speak the truth."

The man picked up his bow and three arrows and he followed his wife. When they came to the edge of the field, the woman pointed.

"Look, over there, beneath the tree."

When the man saw the eagle with his child, he was afraid. He fitted two arrows to his bow and loosed both of them at once.

At that moment the eagle flew up into the air and the two arrows pierced the child.

The eagle circled in the air above the field, crying and keening, and then it spoke: "Now is all kindness at an end. Look what you've done. You have rewarded tenderness with death... and from this day onwards there will be murder among men!"

And from that day to this people have killed each other.

Blue Cuckoo, Red-Bellied Coucal

YORUBA

The blue cuckoo

Lays white eggs in the bush.

When war captures the town

The blue cuckoo cries:

"*Kukuku ogun*

Kill twenty, kill twenty!"

The red-bellied coucal cries:

"*Kukuku ogbon*

Kill thirty, kill thirty!"

Then death will not fail to come

Then death will not fail to come.

When men begin war

The blue cuckoo cries:

"Fools, fools!"

The red-bellied coucal cries:

"The world is spoiled

The world is spoiled!"

Then death cannot fail to come

Then death cannot fail to come.

The Songs of the Birds

BRAZILIAN

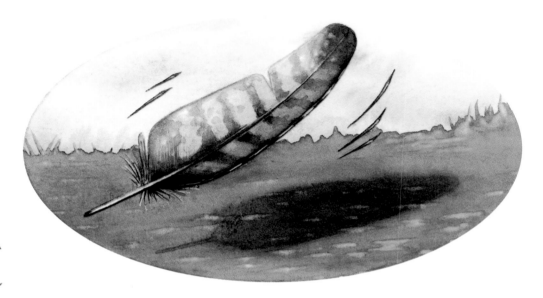

Once everything spoke the same language. People, plants, insects, animals, birds — all shared a single language and understood one another perfectly.

One day a young man was walking in the jungle far from his village and he heard voices. He peered through the trees and saw a village of bird people. They were beautiful with their red and green, their blue and yellow feathers. The elders of the village were sitting and talking. They were so beautiful that the young man was filled with envy. He made his way towards them.

"What do you want, stranger?" said the bird people.

The young man came across and crouched down beside them.

"I would like to be a bird, I would like to dress in feathers and fly high above the tops of the trees like you."

The bird people shook their heads.

"You would not say these things if you knew the truth. Once our lives were sweet, but now things have changed. Death has come. There is a hunter who kills us. He comes with arrows and spears. Toucans, macaws, eagles, even the little hummingbirds have lost their lives. He decorates himself with our feathers, he cooks our flesh over his fire."

The young man said: "What is this hunter's name?"

"He is called Avatsiu."

The young man stood up.

"Avatsiu! I know him. He lives in my village...so, he is a murderer!"

The bird people nodded: this was a new word, they were pleased with the sound of it.

"Listen," said one of them. "If you would help us to get rid of this Avatsiu, then you too could become a bird."

The young man was delighted.

"Yes," he said. "Yes, I'll help you."

The bird people told him to take off his clothes. They smeared his body with sticky stuff, then they began to give him feathers: long wingfeathers for his arms; little bright-colored feathers for his chest and legs.

He walked across to a pool of water and peered down at himself. He was magnificent!

He thought to himself: "If only my wife and son could see me."

"Now," said the chief of the bird people, "flap your wings."

Gently he beat his wings against the air. Not one feather fell out.

"Again."

He beat his wings harder, he could feel his feet lifting. One feather fluttered down to the ground.

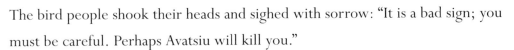

The bird people shook their heads and sighed with sorrow: "It is a bad sign; you must be careful. Perhaps Avatsiu will kill you."

That night the young man stayed in the village of the bird people.

The next morning they led him out of the jungle and up the side of a mountain. When they were standing on a high crag, the chief said: "Now you must learn to fly. Look down and you will see a great rock. Lying on the rock there is a white pebble. Swoop down, snatch up the pebble and bring it back here."

The young man looked down. Far, far, far below him he saw the rock, and the white pebble like a pinprick on the gray stone. He opened his wings, tilted forward and fell against the air. Soon the wind was rushing past him, the world was coming towards him at a terrifying speed. He tried to lift and tilt the wings to break the downward plummet, but it was no good: his outstretched feathery arms were knotting at the shoulders. He flew past the rock and landed in a tangle among the branches of a tree.

Up on the crag the bird people shook their heads and sighed with sorrow: "It is a

bad sign; he will not be able to help us."

But the chief said: "Give him time; he will improve with practice."

The young man scrambled to his feet and beat his wings against the air. He flew up from the forest canopy; he flew up and up until he was standing with the birds again. Over and over he tried, and although he never lifted the white stone, with each downward flight he became more skillful.

That night he returned to the village of the bird people.

On the morning of the following day the young man said: "Now I am ready for Avatsiu."

The chief shook his head.

"Not yet, not yet."

The young man was angry.

"Take me to the rocks above the village; I am ready."

The bird people were uneasy, but they led the young man up to the rocks.

Looking down, he could see Avatsiu's hut far below him.

He beat his feathered arms impatiently against the air.

All morning he waited, and then, at last, he saw Avatsiu come out of his doorway into the sunlight. He was holding his bow in his hand; over his shoulder there was a quiver full of arrows.

The young man leaned forward into the air.

"Wait!" said the chief of the bird people.

But it was too late. The young man was already wheeling down out of the air; he was plummeting down out of the sky.

Avatsiu saw a shadow on the ground before him. He looked up.

Quick as a flash, he fitted an arrow to his bowstring and loosed it.

The young man crashed to the ground at Avatsiu's feet with an arrow embedded

in his feathery chest. Avatsiu seized him by his feet and dragged him through the doorway of his hut.

The young man was never seen again.

The bird people shook their heads and sighed with sorrow: "It was as we feared."

They opened their wings and flew back to their village.

The elders sat down together and talked.

"What shall we do now?"

One bird said: "You know, the young man has a son."

Another said: "Does he?"

"Oh yes, he has a son — he told me so himself. If that boy was to hear that his father had been murdered, then he would want to kill Avatsiu."

The other birds nodded: "It is true, he would want to avenge his father's death."

They decided to send the oxblood bird to tell the boy what had happened to his father. His feathers were so bright that he would be noticed straight away. So the oxblood bird flew out of the jungle and into the village. It stood in the doorway of the dead man's hut.

His wife was the first to see the bird. She called her son: "Look! Look at that bird. He peers at us first with one eye and then the other. He wants to tell us something."

She held out her hand and the oxblood bird flew onto her thumb. It spoke to them and told them what had happened. The boy and his mother stood and listened with tears streaming down their faces.

The bird said to the boy: "Come with me. I will take you to our village. We will teach you to be a bird person, we will help you to avenge your father's death."

The woman put her hand on her son's shoulder.

"Go, my son, go with the oxblood bird. But be careful — do not attack Avatsiu

from the front as your father did. His eyes are as sharp as the points of his arrows.

Attack him from behind, take him by surprise."

The boy nodded, he squeezed his mother's hand, and then he followed the oxblood

bird into the jungle.

When they came to the village of the bird people, everything happened as before.

The boy took off his clothes, he was smeared with sticky stuff and covered with

feathers. When he looked down, his toes had become talons.

"Flap your wings," said the chief.

The boy beat his wings.

"Harder, harder!"

Not one feather fluttered to the ground.

The bird people nodded their heads and laughed: "It is a good sign."

They took him up to the crag. The boy fell into the air, swooped down and snatched up the white pebble. The bird people shouted with delight.

On the third day the chief of the bird people said: "Now you are ready."

They climbed the rocks above the village.

"This is not the right place," said the boy. "I will wait in the tall tree behind Avatsiu's house."

The birds flew down to the tree.

All morning they waited, and at last Avatsiu came out of his door with his bow and his quiver full of arrows. They saw him walk across towards the river to drink some water; his back was towards them.

"This is the moment," whispered the chief of the bird people.

The boy swooped down and, seizing the shoulder of his father's killer with his talons, he beat his wings against the air and tried to lift him.

But Avatsiu was too heavy. Two eagles dived down from the tree and dug their claws into Avatsiu's flesh. Together they lifted him up into the air.

Avatsiu was screaming and kicking.

They lifted him high, high, high into the air.

Avatsiu was begging them to spare his life.

They lifted him higher than the highest crag and then they dropped him.

Avatsiu fell through the air and crashed onto the ground.

His arrows, his bow, his back and his skull were smashed and broken.

The bird people danced a dance of triumph around his body.

Then the elders sat down together to talk and decide what should be done with him.

"I say," said the macaw, "that just as he has eaten our flesh, so we should eat his flesh."

The bird people nodded in agreement and their chief sent out messengers to every corner of the world to invite all the birds to that feast.

And all the birds came, all the birds of the world came, and they drank the blood

of Avatsiu and they ate his flesh. They drank and they ate…but as they were feasting, a change came about: their human language disappeared and each bird found itself speaking its own language — its own song-language.

Out of the blood and flesh of Avatsiu came the speech of the birds — trilling, warbling, croaking, crying, hooting, whistling, chirping and chirruping.

The boy stood and listened and he could not understand.

There was a divide now between the humans and the birds, a gap that could not be bridged.

The boy looked down at his feathers and he knew that they did not belong on his body any longer. He pulled them out until the ground at his feet was bright with them. He put on his clothes. When he looked down, his talons had become toes again.

He made his way through the jungle towards his village. The birds followed him for a while, singing and whistling, but he did not know what they were saying. When he reached his mother's hut, he had a story to tell that would never be forgotten.

And the birds were so delighted with their new languages that they all agreed to go back to their bird villages and raise their voices to the dawn.

And so they flew away from that place; they flew north, south, east and west across the world, and when the sun rose they opened their throats and sang praises to the sky.

And even to this day they sing to the dawn, exulting in the song-languages they took from the blood of Avatsiu.

Magpie Song

NAVAHO

The magpie! The magpie!
Here underneath
in the white of his wings
are the footsteps of morning.
It dawns! It dawns!

The Golden Bird

BEDOUIN

There once lived a wealthy merchant. He had gold and silver and precious stones beyond counting, but his most prized possession was a bird. It was a golden bird that had been trapped by tribesmen far out among the dunes of the desert. The merchant had seen it for sale in a souk and had paid a high price for it. To him it was worth more than all his other wealth. It spoke with such eloquence, it sang with such sweetness, its feathers glowed with such a golden luster that he could not bring himself to let it out of its cage. He loved it as though it was his own child.

He hung the cage in the window of his bed chamber. Every morning and evening he would sit by the bird and listen to its songs to the dawn and the dusk, and he would press little cakes of sesame seed and honey between the golden bars.

And every morning and evening as the bird pecked at the sesame seed, it would say: "Open the door of the cage and let me stretch my wings. Please open the door and let me fly from perch to sill to bedpost to basin…I promise I will return again."

But the merchant would only smile and shake his head: "No, my golden bird, I cannot open the door. What if you were to fly away and break my heart?"

One time the merchant had to make a journey. He was to be away for several weeks. He had instructed his servants to feed the bird during his absence. When everything had been made ready, when his horses and camels were loaded with baggage and waiting for him, he went to his bed chamber to see the bird one last time.

He sat down beside the cage.

"Goodbye, my precious golden bird. I have a great journey to make; I will not see you for a while."

The bird cocked its head on one side, opened its beak, and a melancholy ripple of pure song filled the room.

The merchant got up to leave, and the bird spoke: "Wait, listen. If on your journey you see a ruined city of white stone in the heart of the desert, and if you see a cluster of date palms growing beside it, and if you see on the highest of those trees a bird just like me…then tell her that I am alive. She is my wife, you see. Tell her all about me — and whatever she says or does by way of a reply, remember it and tell me when you return."

The merchant nodded his head: "I promise, if I find that place and see that bird, then I will do all that you ask of me."

And he left the room.

Soon he was traveling across the desert, making his way from the souk of one

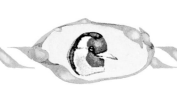

town to the souk of another, buying and selling, bargaining, haggling and
deepening his fortune.

Then, one day, as he was crossing a vast expanse of open sand, he saw a ruined
city of white stone half buried beneath the dunes, and beyond it a cluster of
green palms.

He ordered his men to head towards it.

As soon as they reached the place, the merchant jumped down from his horse and made his way through the ruins to the cluster of date palms.

Sure enough, on the highest branch of the highest tree, there was a golden bird.

He looked up: "Golden bird! I come with news of your husband!"

The golden bird looked down at him and a melancholy ripple of song filled the quiet of the desert.

"He is alive and safe in a golden cage. Every day I feed him with little cakes of sesame seed and honey."

The golden bird nodded its head, then closed its eyes. It swayed on its branch and then fell down through the leaves on to the ground. It lay there without moving. The merchant ran across and looked at it.

The bird was dead. He lifted it gently in his hands. It lay on its back with its legs in the air.

"Poor thing," he whispered. "Poor, beautiful thing."

He scooped up a handful of sand and made a little grave; he set the bird in the grave and covered it over.

Then he made his way back to the horses and camels and the waiting men, his head bowed in sorrow.

As soon as his back was turned, the golden bird fluttered its wings and brushed away the sand. It flew up into the tree and when the merchant was out of sight, it threw back its head and filled the air with rippling peals of laughter.

Some weeks later the merchant returned home. As soon as the horses and camels had been tethered and the men had been paid, he made his way to his bed chamber. The golden bird was hopping from perch to perch in the little cage by the window.

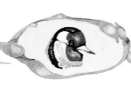

"Ah, my precious golden bird, I am home at last. And I am so happy to see you again."

He sat down beside the cage.

The bird trilled a little song of greeting, then it cocked its head on one side and said: "Did you find the trees by the ruined city?"

The merchant nodded: "I did."

"Did you find my wife on the highest branch of the highest date palm?"

"I did."

"Did you tell her that I am alive?"

"I told her that you are alive and safe in a golden cage."

"And what did she say by way of a reply?"

The merchant shook his head and said nothing.

"What did she say? You must tell me."

The merchant pressed his face against the bars of the cage.

"My precious golden bird, when I told her about you, she fell dead to the ground; she fell stone-dead onto the sand."

The bird looked at the merchant. It closed its eyes and swayed on its perch, then it fell down on to the floor of the cage.

The merchant opened the cage door. The bird was dead. He lifted it in his hands. It lay on its back with its legs in the air.

The merchant carried the bird out of the house. His face and his neck were glistening wet with tears.

"My poor, precious golden bird."

He sat down with the bird on his outstretched hands.

"The news was too much of a shock for you, and now you are dead also."

He set the bird gently on the ground.

"I will make a grave for you."

He got up to fetch a trowel to dig the grave.

As soon as his back was turned, the bird rolled over, stretched its wings and flew up into the sky.

When the merchant returned, it was singing and trilling and filling the air with rippling peals of laughter.

Three times it flew around his head, then it was gone. It was flying across the desert to the ruined city, to the tallest date palm, to the branch where its wife was waiting.

And as for the merchant, he stood with the trowel in his hand and shouted into the sky: "Come back! Ungrateful bird! I loved you as my own child! I fed you with my own hands! And now you fly away and break my heart!"

But the bird was not listening, and why should it? It knew, as we all know, that two birds in the bush are worth a hundred times more than one in the hand!

Swan-Call

SCOTTISH

Guiliog i! Guiliog o!
Guiliog i! Guiliog o!
Guiliog i! Guiliog heard!
Call of the swan, call of the bird!

Call of the swan and she in mist,
Call of the swan and she forlorn,
Call of the swan in early dawn,
Call of the swan the mere-face kist.

Call of the swan and she at sea,
Call of the swan and coldness there,
Call of the swan and biting air,
Call of the swan and she at sea.

My one foot black, my one foot black,
My one foot black with marching track;
My one foot black, where stream-mouth flows,
My other wounded plashing goes.

The Hunter and the Sparrow

AFGHAN

There was once a hunter. He was lazy and careless, so the traps and snares he set were rarely filled.

One morning he got up late and went out into the forest. He checked one trap and then another — all of them were empty. The more traps he checked, the deeper his heart sank in his breast and the louder his belly rumbled with hunger. All morning he made his way along the tracks between the trees. Then suddenly he heard a sound. He heard a panicky chirruping, a battering of wings against leaves. He ran across and crouched down among the bushes.

He'd caught something! It was a sparrow.

He'd caught a little brown sparrow.

"Oh well, you're better than nothing. I'll have you for breakfast!"

He loosened the loop of wire from its leg and took the little bird into his hand.

He smiled at it.

"I'll wring your neck, then I'll pluck you and roast you, my tasty little friend."

The sparrow looked at the hunter, first with one eye then with the other.

"Wait!" it said. "Wait: if you kill me and eat me, the meat you nibble from my bones will only satisfy you for a little while. In half an hour you'll be hungry again. But if you set me free, I'll tell you three truths that you'll remember as long as you live."

The hunter thought to himself: "The bird is right: it's hardly worth the trouble of plucking and roasting for half a mouthful…and a truth is a truth after all, and usually worth having."

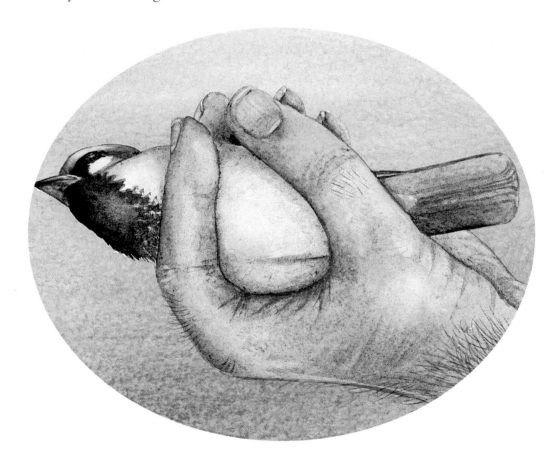

He opened his hand and the sparrow flew up onto a branch above his head.

"My first truth is this: it is a waste of time listening to tales told by liars."

The hunter nodded his head.

"That is good advice; I will always bear it in mind."

The bird flew up to the top of a tree.

"My second truth is this: I have in my belly a priceless diamond as big as a blacksmith's fist. If you had killed me and cooked me, you would have found it. Neither you, nor your sons, nor your grandsons would have ever been hungry again."

The hunter beat his head with his fist.

"What a fool I am: why did I listen to your pleading, why did I set you free?"

He seized his bow and loosed an arrow at the bird.

But the bird was fluttering and flying high above the hunter's head.

"Ha, ha, ha, ha! Already you've forgotten my first truth! How could a little bird like me swallow a diamond as big as a blacksmith's fist? My third truth is this: it is a waste of time giving good advice to sleepy men. The seed that lands on sandy ground will never take root and the snare that's set by a fool will always stay empty!"

And the sparrow flew away.

Crowned Crane

BAMBARA

Crowned crane

Powerful crowned crane

Bird of the word

Beautiful crowned crane

You took part in creation

Voice is your gift, n'guma

Speaking the word, you inflect it

You the drum and the stick that beats it.

What you speak is spoken clearly

Ancestor of praise singers, even the tree

Upon which you perch is worthy of commendation.

Speaking of birds, you make the list complete.

Some have big heads and small beaks

Some have big beaks and small heads

But you have self-knowledge, n'guma

It is the creator who personally adorned you.

The beginning of beginning rhythm

Is speech of the crowned crane;

The crowned crane says, "I speak,"

The word is beauty.

About the Birds

The Golden-Eye Hatches the World — *Finnish*

The idea that the world was formed from an egg is found in many cultures. In Egyptian myth the egg was laid by a goose, the "Great Cackler," the chick was a phoenix, and the two halves of the shell separated the waters of chaos and formed a space in which the creator could make the world. In the Greek "Pelasgian" creation story all the things that exist tumbled out of a "Universal Egg" laid by a dove, while in the Indian Brahmanas (ancient Hindu texts), a golden egg was produced by the primal waters, and out of it hatched Prajapati who named the world into being.

The egg is a powerful symbol for the emergence of life out of apparent stonelike lifelessness. It is no coincidence that at Easter we break open chocolate eggs to celebrate both the coming of spring out of winter and the resurrection from the dead.

The Eagle Above Us — *Cora*

The bird in this poem is the golden eagle. It is venerated by many of the First Nation peoples of America. Its feathers composed the war flag of the Creeks, and among the Dakotas the feathers could be worn only by the warrior who was the first to touch an enemy corpse. Among the Zuni of New Mexico four golden eagle feathers represented the four winds when the rain god was being invoked.

The bald eagle, on the other hand, was not held in high esteem by the Native Americans. When it was chosen in 1782 as the emblem of the United States, even Benjamin Franklin had to admit that

He is a bird of bad moral character; he does not get his living honestly; you may have seen him perched on some dead tree, where, too lazy to fish for himself, he watches the labor of the fishing hawk, and when that diligent bird has at length taken a fish and is bearing it to its nest the bald eagle pursues him and takes it from him... (E. Ingersoll, *Birds in Legend, Fable and Folklore*)

Franklin himself favored the wild turkey, but he was outvoted — and the rest is history.

The Pigeon, the Sparrow-Hawk and the Theft of Fire — *Australian Aboriginal*

According to ancient belief, every Australian Aborigine has a totem; it might be an emu or a witchetty grub, it might be a dingo or a crocodile, or even fire. And every totem is linked to a story. The Australian landscape is full of such stories; every inch of the vast continent, every mountain, hill and water-hole, is connected with one story or another. When a pregnant woman first feels her baby kicking in her womb, she looks about herself very carefully. If she is in a place that is associated with emu stories then she knows that her baby is of the emu totem. This means that the emu is the child's spirit ancestor. She believes that the emu totem has risen up from the land and given the unborn baby its life. From the day the baby is born, the emu stories will be especially sacred to him or her, as will the places that are linked to those stories. And the child will be very careful about eating the flesh of the emu, never to undertake it lightly – because when he does, he will be eating part of himself.

This story about the stealing of fire will be especially sacred to the members of the collared sparrow-hawk totem, the crested pigeon totem and the fire totem. Like most of the Aboriginal tales, it is a story about the "dreaming," a time when the world was still forming itself and everything was in a state of flux and change.

The Birds of Rhiannon — *Celtic*

Throughout Celtic myth there is a pervasive sense of another world just out of reach, just behind or beyond the visible, tangible world. It is the land of perpetual youth — Tir-na-nog or Annwn. It is a place of bright color and delight, of perpetual birdsong, the sound of which brings joy and sleep, heals the weary and can even bring the dead to life. Sometimes in the stories the singing birds of that other world break through the boundaries and visit ours.

When the first Christian missionaries settled in Ireland, the shift from believing in a happy pagan otherworld into an equally happy Christian one was easily made. The singing angels of the plains of heaven are only a flutter away from their pagan prototypes.

The Swallow and the Snake — *Palestinian*

There are many legends and beliefs about the swallow. It is almost always a bird of good omen, probably because its arrival signals the coming of spring. In the Vatican art collection there is a Greek vase, about two and a half thousand years old, that depicts a man and two boys looking up at the sky. The figures have words coming out of their mouths:

First boy: Look, there's a swallow!
Man: By Herakles, so there is!
Second boy (whose arm is raised in a gesture of greeting): There she goes. Spring has come!

In some versions of the story of the bringing of fire, it is the swallow who carries it, burning his head and chest bright red in the process.

There is a Russian tale that tells the story of how, when Jesus was on the cross, the sparrows chirped "Jif! Jif!" (He is living! He is living!) and urged his tormentors to fresh cruelties; while the swallows cried "Umer! Umer!" (He is dead! He is dead!) to try and persuade the tormentors to stop. For this the swallow was blessed and the sparrow cursed. Maybe that is why we have the old rhyme:

The Martin and the Swallow
Are God Almighty's birds to hallow.

It is said to be good luck when a swallow builds its nest under the eaves of the house, but bad luck if it deserts the nest. It is good luck when swallows are flying high, but bad luck when they fly low, especially when they skim between the legs of cattle.

Chicken — *Yoruba*

Although the cockerel enjoys quite an exalted position in myth and folklore as both the bird of the sun and as a bird of augury, the poor hen is best known for her cowardice, her stupidity, as a stickler for hierarchical position…and for her tasty flesh and eggs (sadly the golden ones are nearly always laid by geese). Her one redeeming quality is her motherliness; in Christian iconography she represents the "Mother Church."

The Raven and the Whale — *Inuit*

All over the world the raven is revered for his cunning and for his capacity to survive. Among the Inuit and the First Nation peoples of the north-west coast of America he is a "trickster" (like Coyote and Hare) whose exploits and blunders and unquenchable appetites make things happen and bring things into being. Raven has no moral scruples but there is something both heroic and hilarious about his adventures and escapades.

In northern Europe the raven was sacred to the Celts and the Vikings. The giant Celtic god/king Bran (whose name means "raven") decreed that his head should be buried beneath the "White Hill" in London. The "White Hill" is now "Tower Hill" and ravens are kept there still. Odin, the chief of the Norse gods, had a raven on either shoulder, one called Hugin (which means "thought") and the other Munin (which means "memory"). The idea of thought and memory as two birds, visiting distant places and returning, is quite common in Germanic and Celtic poetry. It brings to mind the raven that was released by Noah and ranged "forth and fro" over the waters of the flood.

Because of its taste for carrion and rotten flesh, the raven is often associated with the field of battle; this is beautifully expressed in the ballad of the "Twa' Corbies":

Ye'll sit on his white head-bone
And I'll pick out his bonny blue een
With a lock of his golden hair
We'll theek our nest when it grows bare

Many a one for him makes moan
But none shall know where he is gone
O'er his white bones, when they're picked bare
The wind shall blow forever mair.

Song for the Vulture Dance — *Orissa*

As with the raven, there is an ambivalence about the vulture. Opinion seems to be almost equally divided as to whether it is a bird of good or evil omen. I am persuaded of the former on the strength of one bird: Jatayu. In the epic Indian story the Ramayana it is Jatayu, the sixty-thousand-year-old king of the birds, who attacks the ten-headed demon Ravana when he steals the beautiful and noble Sita from Prince Rama. Despite his great and venerable age, Jatayu nearly defeats the demon king, but finally Ravana cuts off his wings. The vulture's death, in the arms of Rama, is one of the saddest and most beautiful moments in world mythology.

The King of the Birds — *Inuit*

Variants of this story appear all over Europe and North America. In southern Europe and the Near East, ever since the time of the Sumerian civilization (five thousand years ago), the eagle has been associated with kingship, with light and with the powers of the sky. It was the bird sacred to the father of the Greek pantheon of gods, Zeus (and his Roman counterpart, Jupiter). When the Romans invaded Britain, their legions carried eagle standards.

The tiny wren, on the other hand, was a sacred bird of the Celts, particularly of the druids (it is sometimes called the "druid bird"). It was considered to be a bird of augury, the place that it sang from determining who or what might be on its way: "If it call from the north-west a noble hero of good lineage is coming…if it call from the south, sickness or wolves among your herds" (Anne Ross, *Pagan Celtic Britain*). It was valued also for the way its whole body is consumed with song when it sings. In many parts of Britain there has been a tradition of hunting the wren at midwinter, and parading its body from house to house with great ceremony, singing such verses as:

We have traveled many miles
Over hedges and stiles
In search of our king
Unto you we bring.

The wren was probably the king of the waning year, displaced at midwinter by the robin who was the king of the waxing year. The "Death of Cock Robin" might be a folk memory of the equivalent midsummer sacrifice.

Could it be that the story "The King of the Birds" is an account of an ancient conflict of belief between the south and the north, between Roman and Celt? Or does it just reflect our delight at seeing the little outwit the large? I do not know…but it is said (by the Roman historian Suetonius) that a wren predicted the death of Julius Caesar.

Bird Song — *Copper Eskimo*

The owl of this poem and the previous story is a bird that has many associations. In much American First Nation mythology the owl is a mediator between this world and the world of the ancestors – and it carries gossip and news from our world to theirs.

The little owl was sacred to the Greek goddess Athene ("owl-eyed" Athene) and is associated with wisdom. The short-eared owl, on the other hand, was considered by the Greeks to be a fool (its Greek name "otus" also means "simpleton"). It was said that if you walked around and around a short-eared owl, it would turn its head to follow the movement until it ended up wringing its own neck!

The association of owls with both wisdom and stupidity still continues, but perhaps the strongest association is with evil and the supernatural. This is partly to do with their calls in the night, the t-wit t-woo of the tawny owl and the screech of the barn owl. It is partly because there is a human quality to the face of the owl, as though it is a malevolent spirit following us with its eyes. And it is partly because of the slow, soundless flight of owls — especially the pale barn and snowy owls — like specters in the half-light. (The dusk is sometimes called "owl-light.") Because of their supernatural associations, these beautiful creatures have been unfairly persecuted over the centuries.

The tawny owl's cry is actually a courting song, "t-wit" being the call and "t-wooooo" the response. It is only heard in its entirety during the breeding season; for the rest of the year tawny owls just "t-wit."

The barn owl, one of my favorite birds, has many names: Billy Wise, Madge Howlett, Cherubim, Hobby Owl, Berthuan, Gil-jooter…but the best of all is the Gaelic "Cailleach-oidhche Gheal," which means "White Old Woman of the Night."

The Eagle and the Child — *Baila*

This is a story about the end of a state of grace that existed between the people and the birds. Every culture has its variation on the "Eden" story, in which humankind becomes separated from a "oneness" with the created world. In this story Adam and Cain seem to be combined in the character of the mistrustful father.

There is an ancient association between eagles and babies. According to medieval physicians, a female eagle could not lay her eggs unless she had an "eagle stone" in her nest. If such a stone could be stolen and given to a human mother, it would ensure a safe delivery and a healthy baby. There is also a North African (Berber) belief in a breasted eagle that will suckle human babies in the night. One breast will make the child healthy, the other will cause its death. Maybe it was the fear of a similar bird that caused the father in this tale to loose his two arrows.

Blue Cuckoo, Red-Bellied Coucal — *Yoruba*

This poem is a duet between two different types of African cuckoo, both of whom make the same "ku ku ku" sound. The word "iku" in the Yoruba language means "death," so the refrain "kukuku" means "death, death, death."

In Europe there is a similar tradition: the number of "cuckoos" you hear on "cuckoo day" (the day in spring on which the cuckoo first appears) indicates the number of years that will pass before you die. It can also indicate the number of years until you marry, or the number of children you will have, so its associations are only as morbid as you choose to make them. In fact the cuckoo, throughout Europe, is primarily associated with the joy of the coming of spring, best exemplified in this lovely thirteenth-century song:

Summer is icumen in
Llude sing cuccu
Spryngeth sed and bloweth mede
And groweth the wude new.

According to official ornithological nomenclature, the blue cuckoo and the red-bellied coucal do not exist (the poem is a direct translation from the Yoruba language). I would guess that the blue cuckoo is, in fact, the "yellow-billed cuckoo," which has a beautiful glossy blue-green back and tail, and the red-bellied coucal is the "gabon coucal," which has a rufous belly and underparts. Both birds are to be found in West Africa.

The Songs of the Birds — *Brazilian*

This is another story about the end of a state of grace between the people and the birds, but it is about much more besides. Both father and son are initiated into the spirit world of the birds. For the father this is not appropriate; he is not sufficiently gifted, and he is too impatient and hasty — as a result, he is killed. For the son it *is* appropriate. The indigenous people of Brazil, listening to the story, would have understood this. The way of the shaman is not for everyone.

It is interesting that the divide between birds and humans does not come when Avatsiu kills the birds, but when the birds kill Avatsiu and feast upon his flesh and blood. Perhaps the enmity has to run both ways for the gap to be unbridgeable.

In all my books of birds I can find no reference to the ox-blood bird. Could it be the red macaw (or guacamaya) which was sacred to the Mayan people of Guatemala and the Musicas of Colombia? The red macaw was associated with the worship of the sun, particularly venerated at midsummer, and sometimes called "fire bird."

Further north, in Central America, the quetzal (or trogon) was venerated by the Aztecs in a similar manner. It was sacred to Quetzalcoatl, who ruled the realm where the sun shines at night. The quetzal is considered to be one of the loveliest birds in the world: its crested head and body (roughly sparrow-sized) are iridescent green, its breast and under parts crimson, its wings are black, and its tail (whose saber-shaped feathers are 10 inches long) is bluish green.

Magpie Song — *Navaho*

The magpie, being both black and white, is seen as containing both the dark and the light. In this Navaho poem it separates day from night; in Australian Aboriginal myths it separates the sky from the earth. In medieval legend it is described as being a cross between a raven and a dove (with qualities of both). Perhaps this pied (mixed) character is clearest in the old rhyme "One for sorrow, two for joy."

The Golden Bird — *Bedouin*

I do not know which golden bird this story refers to, but it could be the goldfinch, a bird that is found across Europe and in North Africa. It is favored as a cage-bird more than any other, partly because of its beautiful plumage and partly because of its tinkling conversational song. The song is so beguiling that the collective term for a number of goldfinches is a "charm."

In the English slang of the eighteenth century the term "goldfinch" was used to describe a rich man, perhaps because he flashed his gold as a goldfinch flashes the golden feathers of its wings, perhaps because he was easily trapped!

Swan-Call — *Scottish*

The Anglo-Saxon word "swan" is derived from the word meaning "to sound." The sound of the swan lies not in its call (except for hissing and grunting, it is quite silent) but in the distinctive soughing sound of its flight. In the Anglo-Saxon *The Exeter Book Riddles* the swan riddle reads:

…My white pinions
resound very loudly, ring with a melody,
sing out clearly when I sleep not on
the soil or settle on gray waters — a traveling spirit.

Celtic mythology is full of transformations between human and swan forms. We find them in the Cu Chulainn stories (*The Tain*), in the stories "Midir and Etain" and "The Children of Lir," as well as in countless folk and wonder tales. Similar stories appear across Europe and Asia. They are the traces of an ancient shamanic tradition in which birds were seen as beings from a spirit world, and it was understood that by taking "bird form" it was possible to have access to that world.

Geese and swans (especially the migrating whooper and bewick swans), because of their beauty, their mysterious seasonal comings and goings, their powerful flight, and their ease on water, land and in the air, were especially venerated as spirit beings.

Until quite recently there was a folk belief that the souls of the dead were transformed into swans. Within living memory an old woman on the Scottish island of Uist was said to have been convinced that a wounded swan on Loch Bee was her grandmother.

The Hunter and the Sparrow — *Afghan*

The sparrow is the most familiar of birds, the companion of every household. Because it is small and considered undistinguished (though in fact its feathers are rather lovely), it is often used as a metaphor for the most disposable and worthless of lives, and correspondingly (in Christian lore) as a symbol of God's care for the humblest of his creatures. In the gospel of Matthew (10: 29) Jesus says, "Are not two sparrows sold for a farthing? And one of them shall not fall on the ground without your Father." The Anglo-Saxon chronicler the Venerable Bede must have had these associations in his mind when he wrote in his *Ecclesiastical History*:

Man's life is like a sparrow that steals into the feasting hall and is seen to flit safe from the storm. Here it entered, there on hasty wing it flies out, it passes on from cold to cold; from whence it came we do not know, nor do we behold whither it goes.

In the story "The Hunter and the Sparrow" there is a poignancy in the contrast between the humble sparrow and the wealth that it pretends to carry.

Crowned Crane — *Bambara*

This bird, according to Bambara myth, taught people to speak by giving them the fourteen consonants and five vowels of their language. The trumpet-like sound of the crane's voice represents the inflection of speech, the beautiful plumage of the bird represents the word made manifest (there's a Dogon saying: "To be naked is to be speechless"), and the crane's dance during the mating season represents the rhythm of speech. The bird is an embodiment of the mystery of language.

Sources and Acknowledgements

The Golden-Eye Hatches the World
There are many translations of the Finnish national epic the *Kalevala*. My favorite is by Francis Peabody Magoun, Jr. (Harvard University Press, Cambridge, MA, 1963).

The Eagle Above Us
Translated by Anselm Hollo, from *Shaking the Pumpkin: Traditional Poetry of the Indian North Americas*, edited by Jerome Rothenburg (Alfred Van Der Marck Editions, New York, 1986).

The Pigeon, the Sparrow-Hawk and the Theft of Fire
My source for this story is a anthology of Aboriginal stories collected by Daisy Bates in southern Australia in the 1920s. The book is called *Tales Told to Kabbarli* (Angus and Robertson, Melbourne, 1972). The best collection of Australian Aboriginal stories is *The Speaking Land* by Ronald and Catherine Berndt (Inner Traditions International, Vermont, 1994).

The Birds of Rhiannon
I've drawn together the other-world birds associated with two parallel Celtic goddesses, the Welsh Rhiannon and the Irish Clidna. I'm indebted to Robin Williamson (a fine storyteller and an authority on Celtic tales and poetry) for the attributes of the birds. The best book on this subject is *Pagan Celtic Britain* by Anne Ross (Constable, London, 1992).

The Swallow and the Snake
I first found this clever apocryphal tale in Inea Bushnaq's *Arab Folktales* (Penguin Folklore Library, Harmondsworth, 1987). I've since heard several storytellers telling variants of it.

Chicken
Translated by Ulli Beier, from *The Rattle Bag*, edited by Ted Hughes and Seamus Heaney (Faber & Faber, London, 1982); originally from *Yoruba Poetry* by Ulli Beier (Cambridge University Press, Cambridge, 1970).

The Raven and the Whale
My version of this story owes something to Tom Lowenstein's *Ancient Land: Sacred Whale* (Bloomsbury, London, 1993), something to Alan Garner's *The Guizer* (Hamish Hamilton, London, 1975) and quite a lot to Gail Robinson and Douglas Hill's *Coyote the Trickster* (Piccolo, London, 1981), an excellent introduction for children to the trickster in Native American mythology.

Song for the Vulture Dance
Translated by Verrier Elwin, from *The Unwritten Song* by Willard R. Trask (Jonathan Cape, London, 1969).

The King of the Birds
This widespread story (there is even an Abnaki version of it) seems to have as many variants as there are storytellers. I've known it since I was a boy, though I'm grateful to my friend and fellow storyteller Eric Maddern for reminding me about the cup of tears. For more Welsh stories, Gwyn Jones's *Welsh Legends and Folk-Tales* is a good place to begin (Puffin, Harmondsworth, 1979).

Bird Song
From *Eskimo Poems from Canada and Greenland*, translated by Tom Lowenstein (Allison and Busby, London, 1973).

The Eagle and the Child
I first found this story in Paul Radin's seminal *African Folktales* (Schocken Books, New York, 1983).

Blue Cuckoo, Red-Bellied Coucal
This poem is from *Yoruba Poetry* by Ulli Beier. I'm indebted to Judith Gleason (see "The Crowned Crane") for her notes on the poem.

The Songs of the Birds
This strange and beautiful story I found in *Central and South*

American Stories by Robert Hull (Wayland Publishers, Hove, 1994). I've juggled it about to give it more of an oral symmetry.

Magpie Song

Translated by Washington Matthews, from *The Unwritten Song* by Willard R. Trask (Jonathan Cape, London, 1969).

The Golden Bird

I heard this story from my friend Duncan Williamson, who in turn heard it from a Bedouin storyteller. There is a version of it in Idries Shah's *Tales of the Dervishes* (Panther, St Albans, 1973).

Swan-Call

From *Poems of the Western Highlanders* by G. R. D. McLean (SPCK, London, 1961).

The Hunter and the Sparrow

I heard this Sufi story from Marita Fochler, a Bavarian storyteller. A version of it can be found in Idries Shah's *Tales of the Dervishes*. It has been attributed to the thirteenth-century poet and mystic Jalaludin Rumi.

The Crowned Crane

This African praise poem is from a wonderful book, *Leaf and Bone*, by Judith Gleason (Penguin Books, Harmondsworth, 1994).

About the Birds

I am indebted to Francesca Greenoak's excellent book *British Birds, their Folklore, Names and Literature* (A. & C. Black, London, 1997) for some of the more obscure information that I incorporated in this section of notes on the birds.

Bibliography

Abram, David, *The Spell of the Sensuous*, Random House, New York, 1996.

Bruun, B., *Birds of Britain and Europe*, Hamlyn, London, 1976.

Buck, William, *Ramayana*, University of California Press, Berkeley, CA, 1981.

Child, F. J., *The English and Scottish Popular Ballads*, Dover Publications, New York, 1965.

Cowan, James, *Mysteries of the Dream-Time*, Prism Press, Bridport, 1979.

Crossley-Holland, Kevin (tr.), *The Exeter Book Riddles*, Penguin, Harmondsworth, 1979.

Davy, Marie-Madeleine, *L'Oiseau et sa symbolique*, Editions Albin Michel, Paris, 1998.

Del Hogo, J., Elliott, A. and Sargatal, J. (eds), *Handbook of the Birds of the World*, Lynx Editions, Barcelona, 1994.

Flegg, J. and Madge, S., *Birds of Australia*, New Holland, London, 1995.

Harris, G., *Gods and Pharoahs from Egyptian Mythology*, Eurobook, London, 1982.

Hawkes, Jacquetta, *A Land*, Cresset Press, London, 1951.

Howard, R. and Moore, A., *A Complete Checklist of the Birds of the World*, Academic Press, London, 1991.

Ingersoll, E., *Birds in Legend, Fable and Folklore*, Longmans, Green and Co., New York, 1923.

March, J., *Dictionary of Classical Mythology*, Cassell, London, 1998.

Orchard, A., *Dictionary of Norse Myth and Legend*, Cassell, London, 1998.

Radin, Paul, *The Trickster*, Schocken Books, New York, 1972.

Ross, Anne, *Pagan Celtic Britain*, Constable, London, 1992.

Sproul, Barbara, *Primal Myths*, Harper & Row, New York, 1979.